For Jack, Olivia, Lily, and Nicholas,
who give me countless reasons to be grateful.—A. C. R.

For Claire and Oli.

With special thanks to Kristen.—I. H.

Text copyright © 2018 Annie Cronin Romano
Illustrations copyright © 2018 Ioana Hobai

First published in 2018 by Page Street Kids,
an imprint of
Page Street Publishing Co.
27 Congress Street, Suite 105
Salem, MA 01970
www.pagestreetpublishing.com

Distributed by Macmillan, sales in Canada by The Canadian Manda Group

18 19 20 21 22 CCO 5 4 3 2 1

ISBN-13: 978-1-62414-578-0
ISBN-10: 1-624-14578-7

CIP data for this book is available from the Library of Congress.

This book was typeset in Amasis MT and Argentile.
The illustrations were done in mixed media (graphite, colored pencil, and watercolor).

Printed and bound in China

Page Street Publishing uses only materials from suppliers who are committed to responsible and sustainable forest management.

Page Street Publishing protects our planet by donating to nonprofits like
The Trustees, which focuses on local land conservation.

# BEFORE YOU
## Sleep

### A BEDTIME BOOK OF GRATITUDE

Annie Cronin Romano    illustrated by Ioana Hobai

PAGE
STREET
KiDS

Before you quiet down your mind,
recall the sounds you leave behind.

The scratching of the sidewalk chalk,
birds chirping in the trees,

the bouncy beat of songs you've sung,
a whisper in the breeze.

The squeaking of the front door hinge,
your sister's happy laugh,
the clatter in the kitchen sink,
splish-splashing in your bath.

Replay the sounds of daytime's theme
before you sleep, before you dream.

Before you rest your head to doze,
recall the scents that filled your nose.

Your parents' coffee in their cups,
strawberries in the field,

the smell of Grandpa's aftershave,
ripe orange, freshly peeled.

The scent of neighbor's fresh-cut lawn,
spring lilacs all in bloom,
the stink of baby's diaper,
and the smell of Mom's perfume.

Breathe in the scents of daytime's scene
before you sleep, before you dream.

Before you say that day is done,
recall the tastes that graced your tongue.

A sour sip of lemonade,
grape jelly on your toast,

a chocolate bar you chose yourself,
that snack you love the most.

The veggies that you just can't stand
but Mom insists you eat,
the salty crunch of crackers,
cherry slushy, cold and sweet.

Give thanks for tastes as rich as cream
before you sleep, before you dream.

Before you drift into night's haze,
remember sights that met your gaze.

The glare of sunshine on the lake,
the sparkle of the rain,

crisp apples in their coats of red,
gray rocks along the lane.

The smile on your best friend's face,
wool mittens, bright and blue,
the pictures in your favorite book,
a gift wrapped just for you.

Be grateful for what you have seen
before you sleep, before you dream.

Before into night's sleep you melt,
remember all that you have felt.

A kitten's fur as smooth as silk,
your blanket soft and warm,

snow's icy chill upon your cheek,
hot cocoa through the storm.

The bear hug from a friend so true,
the stubble on Dad's chin,
an itchy sweater all worn out,
sun's kiss upon your skin.

Be thankful for life's touch supreme
before you sleep, before you dream.

Before the sun slips to the west,
tuck in your senses snug to rest.

Let heavy eyelids close to find
the stars that light the sky,

the smell of minty toothpaste,

and a peaceful lullaby.

Enjoy just one more bedtime drink,
then cuddle on cool sheets.

Let cricket sounds and honeyed scents
fill up the night's heartbeats.

Collect these joys and watch them gleam
before you sleep, before you dream.